BRINGING THE RAIN TO KAPITI PLAIN

A Nandi Tale

BRINGING THE RAIN TO KAPITI PLAIN

PLAIN *retold by Verna Aardema / pictures by Beatriz Vidal*

Dial Books for Young Readers / New York

Published by
Dial Books for Young Readers
A division of Penguin Young Readers Group
345 Hudson Street, New York, New York 10014

Text copyright © 1981 by Verna Aardema
Pictures copyright © 1981 by Beatriz Vidal
Manufactured in China
COBE
20 19 18

The full-color artwork is painted in gouache in order to achieve a flat effect.
It is then camera-separated and reproduced in four-color process.

Bringing the Rain to Kapiti Plain is retold from
"The Nandi House That Jack Built" in Alfred C. Hollis's book
The Nandi: Their Language and Folklore, Oxford, Eng.: Clarendon Press, 1909.

Library of Congress Cataloging in Publication Data
Aardema, Verna. Bringing the rain to Kapiti Plain.
Summary: A cumulative rhyme relating how Ki-pat
brought rain to the drought-stricken Kapiti Plain.
[1. Droughts—Fiction. 2. Africa—Fiction.
3. Stories in rhyme] I. Vidal, Beatriz. II. Title.
PZ8.3.A123Br [E]   80-25886
ISBN 0-8037-0809-2
ISBN 0-8037-0807-6 (lib. bdg.)

For my librarian,
Bernice Houseward
V. A.

For my parents; for my teacher
B. V.

This is the great
　　Kapiti Plain,
All fresh and green
　　from the African rains—
A sea of grass for the
　　ground birds to nest in,
And patches of shade for
　　wild creatures to rest in;
With acacia trees for
　　giraffes to browse on,
And grass for the herdsmen
　　to pasture their cows on.

But one year the rains
    were so very belated,
That all of the big wild
    creatures migrated.
Then Ki-pat helped to end
    that terrible drought—
And this story tells
    how it all came about!

This is the cloud,
    all heavy with rain,
That shadowed the ground
    on Kapiti Plain.

This is the grass,
   all brown and dead,
That needed the rain
   from the cloud overhead—
The big, black cloud,
   all heavy with rain,
That shadowed the ground
   on Kapiti Plain.

These are the cows,
    all hungry and dry,
Who mooed for the rain
    to fall from the sky;
To green-up the grass,
    all brown and dead,
That needed the rain
    from the cloud overhead—
The big, black cloud,
    all heavy with rain,
That shadowed the ground
    on Kapiti Plain.

This is Ki-pat,
  who watched his herd
As he stood on one leg,
  like the big stork bird;
Ki-pat, whose cows
  were so hungry and dry,
They mooed for the rain
  to fall from the sky;
To green-up the grass,
  all brown and dead,
That needed the rain
  from the cloud overhead—
The big, black cloud,
  all heavy with rain,
That shadowed the ground
  on Kapiti Plain.

This is the eagle
    who dropped a feather,
A feather that helped
    to change the weather.
It fell near Ki-pat,
    who watched his herd
As he stood on one leg,
    like the big stork bird;
Ki-pat, whose cows
    were so hungry and dry,
They mooed for the rain
    to fall from the sky;
To green-up the grass,
    all brown and dead,
That needed the rain
    from the cloud overhead—
The big, black cloud,
    all heavy with rain,
That shadowed the ground
    on Kapiti Plain.

This is the arrow
        Ki-pat put together,
With a slender stick
        and an eagle feather;
From the eagle who happened
        to drop a feather,
A feather that helped
        to change the weather.

It fell near Ki-pat,
   who watched his herd
As he stood on one leg,
   like the big stork bird;
Ki-pat, whose cows
   were so hungry and dry,
They mooed for the rain
   to fall from the sky;
To green-up the grass,
   all brown and dead,
That needed the rain
   from the cloud overhead—
The big, black cloud,
   all heavy with rain,
That shadowed the ground
   on Kapiti Plain.

This is the bow,
    so long and strong,
And strung with a string,
    a leather thong;
A bow for the arrow
    Ki-pat put together,
With a slender stick
    and an eagle feather;
From the eagle who happened
    to drop a feather,
A feather that helped
    to change the weather.

It fell near Ki-pat,
　　who watched his herd
As he stood on one leg,
　　like the big stork bird;
Ki-pat, whose cows
　　were so hungry and dry,
They mooed for the rain
　　to fall from the sky;
To green-up the grass,
　　all brown and dead,
That needed the rain
　　from the cloud overhead—
The big, black cloud,
　　all heavy with rain,
That shadowed the ground
　　on Kapiti Plain.

This was the shot
    that pierced the cloud
And loosed the rain
    with thunder LOUD!
A shot from the bow,
    so long and strong,
And strung with a string,
    a leather thong;
A bow for the arrow
    Ki-pat put together,
With a slender stick
    and an eagle feather;
From the eagle who happened
    to drop a feather,
A feather that helped
    to change the weather.

It fell near Ki-pat,
    who watched his herd
As he stood on one leg,
    like the big stork bird;
Ki-pat, whose cows
    were so hungry and dry,
They mooed for the rain
    to fall from the sky;
To green-up the grass,
    all brown and dead,
That needed the rain
    from the cloud overhead—
The big, black cloud,
    all heavy with rain,
That shadowed the ground
    on Kapiti Plain.

So the grass grew green,
and the cattle fat!
And Ki-pat got a wife
and a little Ki-pat—

Who tends the cows now,
    and shoots down the rain,
When black clouds shadow
    Kapiti Plain.

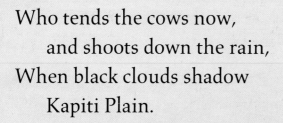

About the Author

Verna Aardema is a highly acclaimed storyteller and the author of many books of African folktales. Her most recent book for Dial, *Who's in Rabbit's House?*, illustrated by Leo and Diane Dillon, was an American Library Association Notable Children's Book and a *School Library Journal* Best Book of the Year, 1977. *Why Mosquitoes Buzz in Péople's Ears*, also illustrated by the Dillons, was awarded the Caldecott Medal in 1976 and was chosen as an American Library Association Notable Children's Book, as was a third Aardema-Dillon collaboration, *Behind the Back of the Mountain*.

Ms. Aardema was born in New Era, Michigan, and received her degree in journalism from Michigan State University. She now lives in Muskegon, Michigan, with her husband, Dr. Joel Vugteveen.

About the Artist

Beatriz Vidal was born in Argentina and received her Bachelor of Arts from Córdoba University. She has studied art with Ilonka Karasz, and her illustrations have appeared on UNICEF cards and publications including *Vogue* and *Woman's Day*.

Ms. Vidal currently lives in New York City. This is her first children's book.

About the Tale

This tale was discovered in Kenya, Africa, more than seventy years ago by the famous anthropologist Sir Claud Hollis. Sir Claud camped near a Nandi village and learned the native language from two young boys. He learned riddles and proverbs from the Nandi children, and most of the folktales from the Chief Medicine Man. This tale reminded Sir Claud of a cumulative nursery rhyme he had loved as a boy in England, one also familiar to us—"The House That Jack Built." So he called the story "The Nandi House That Jack Built" and included it in his book *The Nandi: Their Language and Folklore*, published in 1909. Verna Aardema has brought the original story closer to the English nursery rhyme by putting in a cumulative refrain and giving the tale the rhythm of "The House That Jack Built."